Meet Monkey Boo's Fami[ly]

Mummy Boo

Daddy Boo

Monkey Boo

Little Boo Boo

And Monkey Boo's Friends...

Katie Kangaroo

Ruby Rabbit

Perry Panda

Eddie Elephant

CW01043978

For my precious girls, Nicole and Jolie

WHAT DOES MONKEY BOO LOVE?

Tam Sainsbury

Monkey Boo loves his ears

Monkey Boo loves his nose

Monkey Boo loves his tummy

and Monkey Boo loves his toes

What else does Monkey Boo love?

Monkey Boo loves to play

Monkey Boo loves to hide

Monkey Boo loves the swing

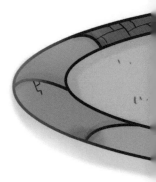

and Monkey Boo loves the slide

What else does Monkey Boo love?

Monkey Boo loves the sun

Monkey Boo loves the rain

Monkey Boo loves the car

and Monkey Boo loves the train

What else does Monkey Boo love?

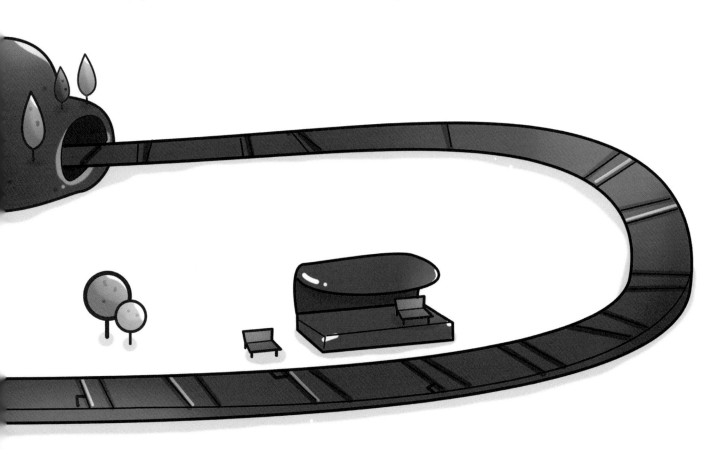

Monkey Boo loves the ducks

Monkey Boo loves his cat

Monkey Boo loves his shoes

and Monkey Boo loves his hat

What else does Monkey Boo love?

Monkey Boo loves his mummy

Monkey Boo loves hugs

Monkey Boo loves his daddy

and Monkey Boo loves bugs

What else does Monkey Boo love?

Monkey Boo loves bananas

Monkey Boo loves bread

Monkey Boo loves the bath

and Monkey Boo loves his bed

But what does Monkey Boo REALLY love?

Turn the page to find out.....

One....

Two...

Monkey Boo loves you!

Printed in Poland
by Amazon Fulfillment
Poland Sp. z o.o., Wrocław